MIA HAMM
Winners Never Quit!

Illustrations by **Carol Thompson**

HarperCollins*Publishers*

Special thanks to Sarah L. Thomson

Winners Never Quit!
Text and illustrations copyright © 2004 by Mia Hamm and Byron Preiss Visual Publications, Inc.
Printed in Mexico

Library of Congress Cataloging-in-Publication Data is available.

Typography by Jeanne L. Hogle
1 2 3 4 5 6 7 8 9 10
❖
First Edition

For my family
—M.H.

For Richard Hunter, with love
—C.T.

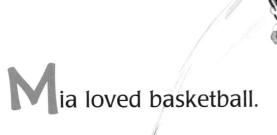

M ia loved basketball.

Mia loved baseball.

But most of all, Mia loved soccer.
She played every day with her
brothers and sisters.

Tap, tap, tap. Her toes kept the ball right where she wanted it.
Then, *smack*! She'd kick the ball straight into the net. *Goal!*
Everybody on her team would cheer.

But sometimes it didn't work that way.
One day, no matter how hard she tried, Mia couldn't score a goal.

The ball sailed to the left of the net.   Or to the right.

Or her sister Lovdy,
the goalie, saved the
ball with her hands.

No goal.

No cheering.

"Too bad, Mia," her brother Garrett said. "Better luck next time!"

But Mia didn't want better luck next time. She wanted better luck *now*.

"You can't quit!" Lovdy said. "Then we'll only have two people on our team."

"Come on, Mia," her sister Caroline pleaded. "You always quit when you start losing."

"Just keep playing, Mia," Garrett said. "It'll be fun."

But losing wasn't fun. Mia stomped back to the house.

"Quitter!" Lovdy yelled.

Mia didn't care.
She'd rather quit than lose.

The next day, Mia ran outside, ready to play soccer. When she got there, the game had already started.

"Hey!" she yelled. "Why didn't you wait for me?"

Garrett stopped playing.

"Sorry, Mia," he said. "But quitters can't play on my team."

"Yeah," said Lovdy. "If you can't learn to lose, you can't play."

Garrett passed the ball to Tiffany.
Martin ran to steal it. Tiffany dashed
around him and took a shot at the goal.
Lovdy blocked it.

Mia just stood
by the side and
watched.

The next day, Garrett picked Mia first for his team.

Mia got the ball. She dribbled down the field. *Smack!* She kicked the ball toward the goal.

And Lovdy caught it.

"Too bad, Mia," Garrett said. "Better luck next time."

Mia felt tears in her eyes.

"She's going to quit," whispered Lovdy. "I *knew* it."

Mia still hated losing. But she didn't hate losing as much as she loved soccer.

"Ready to play?" asked Garrett.
Mia nodded.
Garrett grinned at her. He passed her the ball.

Mia ran down the field. Tap, tap, tap with her toes. The ball stayed right with her, like a friend. She got ready to kick it into the goal.

Mia kicked the ball as hard
as she could.
Maybe she'd score the goal.
Maybe she wouldn't.
But she was playing.

And that was more important than winning or losing…

...because winners never quit!

Hi,

I hope you have enjoyed reading *Winners Never Quit!* While playing soccer with my family, I learned the importance of being part of a team, and how to lose gracefully. Throughout my soccer career, these lessons have helped me succeed. I have often said there is no "me" in Mia because, in soccer and in life, I could never do it alone. Whatever you love to do, remember—winners never quit!

Mia focuses on the goal, with the ball at her feet, at the 2003 Women's World Cup tournament, where it was said she played the best soccer of her career.

In 1979, an eight-year-old Mia (third from left) is playing with the Sidewinders, a team her father, Bill Hamm, coached while their family was stationed at Sheppard Air Force Base in Wichita Falls, Texas.

Mia (center) and her teammates celebrate winning the gold medal in Atlanta at the 1996 Olympic Games in front of 80,000 fans. Prior to this pinnacle moment in her career, Mia was the youngest woman ever to play with the U.S. National Team, at the age of fifteen. She won her first World Cup championship four years later in 1991. In college, she played soccer at the University of North Carolina, where she led her team to four consecutive NCAA championships.

Mia's family was later stationed at Randolph Air Force Base in San Antonio, Texas. This 1981 photo shows her throwing in the ball.

Despite the disappointing loss to Norway in the final game of the 2000 Sydney Olympics, Mia celebrates with her teammates. She helped bring home the silver medal.

Mia scores on a penalty kick against China at the final game of the Women's World Cup in July 1999. After two fifteen-minute overtimes, USA defeated China and took home the World Championship in front of 90,000 soccer fans and more than one billion television viewers worldwide. With forty million viewers in the U.S. alone, it was the highest-rated women's sports event on television in U.S. history. Mia, at twenty-seven, became the world's leading goal scorer in international competition, male or female.

Mia (left) steals the ball from Australian soccer star Julie Murray at the inaugural game of the Women's United Soccer Association (WUSA) in 2001. She was the captain of her team, the Washington Freedom. Two years later, in August 2003, Hamm helped lead the Freedom to what would be the WUSA's last championship.